and BOB

and the Particularly Pesky Attack of the Pencil People

BY **L. Bob Rovetch**   ILLUSTRATED BY **Dave Whamond**

chronicle books · san francisco

Book design by Mary Beth Fiorentino.
Typeset in Clarendon and Agenda.
The illustrations in this book were rendered in ink,
watercolor washes, and Prismacolor.
Manufactured in the United States of America.

Library of Congress Cataloging-in-Publication Data
Rovetch, Lissa.
Hot Dog and Bob and the particularly pesky attack of the Pencil People :
adventure #2 / by L. Bob Rovetch ; illustrated by Dave Whamond.
p. cm.
Summary: Fifth-grader Bob and his best friend Clementine are visited by
the superhero Hot Dog from the planet Dogzalot to warn of an invasion
of evil pencils with plans to erase the whole world.
ISBN-13: 978-0-8118-4464-2 (library edition)
ISBN-10: 0-8118-4464-1 (library edition)
ISBN-13: 978-0-8118-5322-4 (pbk.)
ISBN-10: 0-8118-5322-5 (pbk.)
[1. Pencils—Fiction. 2. Frankfurters—Fiction. 3. Extraterrestrial beings—
Fiction. 4. Schools—Fiction. 5. Humorous stories.] I. Whamond, Dave, ill.
II. Title.
PZ7.R784Hot 2006
[Fic]—dc22
2005026777

Distributed in Canada by Raincoast Books
9050 Shaughnessy Street, Vancouver, British Columbia V6P 6E5

10 9 8 7 6 5 4 3 2

Chronicle Books LLC
85 Second Street, San Francisco, California 94105

www.chroniclekids.com

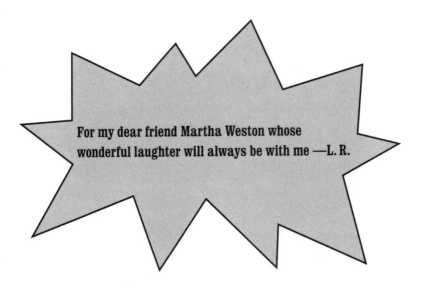

For my dear friend Martha Weston whose
wonderful laughter will always be with me —L. R.

Contents

Chapter 1

Trouble

Want to know the freakiest day of my life? It was the day I opened my lunch box to find a superhero hot dog sitting on top of my pizza.

"Hot Dog's my name, fightin' bad stuff's my game!" said the talking wienie. "It'll be me and you, stickin' like glue. Partners till the very end!"

The next thing I knew, my teacher, Miss Lamphead, had morphed into a huge alien pizza person named Cheese Face. Things got really weird when she turned everybody, including our class hamster, into mutant zombie pizza soldiers.

To make a long story short, everything turned out okay in the end. My classroom went back to normal, Hot Dog went back to his planet, Dogzalot, and my best friend, Clementine, and I were the only ones who remembered that anything weird had even happened.

We promised never to talk about Hot Dog or the whole scary pizza thing ever again. We tried as hard as we could to act like normal kids in a normal school, and if you ask me, we did a pretty good job—until last week, that is.

"Mmmm! Yummylicious!" Clementine said with her mouth full. "Wanna bite?"

I looked at her lunch. It was another one of her usual *un*usual creations: a peanut butter, banana, avocado, red pepper, onion, ham, chocolate chip, cream cheese, raisin, alfalfa sprout and extra hot horseradish on rye bread sandwich. Yummylicious? I don't think so!

"I seriously don't get how you can eat those things without getting sick," I said. But I knew better than anyone that Clementine had a stomach of steel. She could handle even the most repulsive foods.

That's when Clementine broke our sacred promise. She burped and said, "Hey, Bob, don't you ever wish you could see Hot Dog again? You know, just for old times' sake?"

"No way!" I said. "The only time superhero hot dogs show up is when something terrible is about to happen. Asking to see Hot Dog would just be asking for trouble."

"Did someone say *trouble?*" a voice called out from my lunch box.

"Oh, no," I said, lifting the lid. "It can't be!"

But it could be—it was! Smushed between my carrots and my juice box. Looking up at Clementine and me with that crazy gotta-save-the-world kind of look that only superheroes get. Hot Dog was back. I glared at Clementine. If only she hadn't mentioned his name!

"Dude," I whispered into my lunch box. "PLEASE tell me you just popped by to say hello."

"I won't lie to you, partner," said Hot Dog. "You got a heapin' helpin' of trouble on this planet of yours."

"Don't tell me Cheese Face is back!" said Clementine.

"No such luck," said Hot Dog. "This mission is so tough the Big Bun almost sent two of us superhero hot dogs down from Dogzalot."

"Well, why didn't she?" I asked nervously.

"Oh, I convinced her that we could handle it," said Hot Dog.

"W-w-w-we?" I stuttered.

"Between you and me and the little lady here," he said, pointing at Clementine, "we've got it covered. No problem!"

The end-of-lunch bell rang, and I hadn't eaten a single bite.

"Tell me this isn't happening again," I begged Clementine.

"Okay, Bob," she said, rolling her eyes. "This isn't happening again."

But we both knew perfectly well that it *was* happening. And there was nothing either of us mere mortals could do about it.

Chapter 2

Be Afraid, Humans!

"Hurry and take your seats, class," said Miss Lamphead. "It's time for our Thursday spelling test."

I slid my lunch box under my desk and held my breath.

"The first word is *boysenberry*," Miss Lamphead said. "The nice boy made boysenberry jam with his mother. *Boysenberry.*"

"*Yes!*" I thought to myself. "That is *so* easy." And I wrote down the word *boysenberry*. But when I double-checked, it said, "BE AFRAID!"

"The next word," said Miss Lamphead, "is *history*. The history of our country is so fascinating. *History*."

"Another easy one," I thought. But when I wrote it down, it came out "HUMANS!"

"What in the world?" I accidentally blurted out loud.

Every single kid in my class turned around to look at me. I didn't know what was going on with my pencil, but I knew it couldn't be good!

"Is there a problem, Bob?" asked Miss Lamphead.

"No, no problem," I answered, trying to look as unlike someone with a potentially possessed pencil as possible.

"Very well." She continued. "The next word is *invitation*. Geraldo gave Petunia an invitation to his birthday party. *Invitation*."

I tried as hard as I could to write *invitation*, but my pencil had a mind of its own. It went crazy, scribbling the words "PREPARE TO BE

ERASED!!!" I struggled to tackle it. How could a measly little pencil be so strong? Finally I grabbed it by the bottom end, flipped it over and erased. But my messed-up spelling words just got all smudgy. Then everything got all slippery. My pencil was oozing slime all over the place. And to top it off, I could have sworn it was laughing at me.

"Awesome!" said Barfalot, my least favorite person on the face of the Earth. "Bob just puked all over his spelling test!"

"Awesome!" repeated Barfalot's brainless bodyguard brothers, Pigburt and Slugburt. If there was ever a place in the *Guinness Book of World Records* for the meanest, dumbest fifth-grade bullies ever invented, nobody could even begin to compete with the Terrible Triplets.

"Oh, dear, Bob!" said Miss Lamphead. "You'd better go straight to Nurse Bunyan's office!"

I grabbed my lunch box and left, only I didn't go to the nurse's office. I slipped into the janitor's closet and opened my lunch box.

"How come you didn't tell me to watch out for scary slime-spewing pencils?" I asked Hot Dog.

"That ambulance siren of a lunch bell cut me off," said Hot Dog. "I was just getting ready to tell you about our mission when—"

"*Our* mission?" I interrupted. "No way!
Uh-uh. Thanks, but no thanks. I don't want
anything to do with your crazy interplanetary
weirdness!"

"Sorry, kid," said Hot Dog. "But you've got
no choice. If you back out now, the Big Bun's
gonna be hoppin' mad. And believe me, Bobby
boy, you do *not* want to make the Big Bun
mad! Besides, she said you did such a

swell job helping me get rid of Cheese Face she knows she can count on you."

"Really?" I asked. "She said that?"

"Yes siree," Hot Dog answered. "And she had plenty of nice things to say about your spunky little girlfriend, too!"

"Clementine?" I asked.

"She's one smart cookie," said Hot Dog. "Yes indeedy, that one's a keeper. I betcha if you play your cards right, wedding bells'll be ring-a-ding-dingin' for the two of you some day."

"*Eww.* Now I really am gonna throw up."
I gagged. "Clementine and I are just friends.
That is *so* sick."

"Speaking of sick," Hot Dog said, rubbing his
tiny little hands together all excitedly, "where
are you keeping that good-for-nothin' pencil?"

"I'm not *keeping* it anywhere," I said. "It's back
in class, on top of my wrecked spelling test."

"You—you let him go? Tell me you didn't just
let him go! Oh, this is bad, buddy boy. This
is really, really bad!" Hot Dog hopped out of
my lunch box and started pacing around in
circles. "*That,* I'm sorry to say, partner, was not
just any old number-two pencil. *That,* my friend,
was *the Scribbler!*"

"The Scribbler?" I said.

Chapter 3

Pencilvania

"That's right," said Hot Dog. "The Scribbler—the dastardly, dangerous and extremely pointy leader of the Pencil Snatchers gang. They're out to take over the universe, one pencil at a time. They sneak into school desks and beam the ordinary pencils to Pencilvania. Once the regular pencils are out of the way, the pencil snatchers take their place."

"Hold on," I said. "Isn't Pennsylvania a state in America?"

"Different Pencilvania," said Hot Dog. "The Scribbler's Pencilvania is a terrible planet where innocent pencils are forced to live in crowded pencil cases *without any paper at all!"*

As I stood there in the dark, stinky janitor's closet, trying to feel sorry for captive pencils on another planet, I heard footsteps.

"Freeze!" I whispered to Hot Dog. "Someone's coming!"

The door blasted open. Mr. Spudbucket, the school janitor, reached his hand inside the dark closet. "Where's that moldy old mop gone to this time?" he grumbled as he fished around. I tried to dodge his hand, but before I knew

it, he was grabbing my hair and pulling
really, really hard. I stifled a scream and shoved
the mop in his direction. Luckily, he finally
grabbed the mop, slammed the door shut and
walked away.

"Phew! That was close," I said, rubbing my
head. "Now, how about *I* go home and *you* save
the world without me?"

"Sorry, kid," said Hot Dog. "The Big Bun
wants you in on this deal. Did you forget? You're
the one who's supposed to remember the plan!"

In the old days, before I'd ever heard of superhero hot dogs and evil dudes from other planets, I was actually kind of proud of having a good memory. But ever since I met my so-called partner, Mr. No Memory, it didn't seem all that lucky anymore.

"If we don't hurry back to that classroom," Hot Dog said, climbing inside my lunch box, "you might not have a *home* to go home *to!*"

I wanted to go back to class about as much as a turkey wants to be the guest of honor at a

Thanksgiving dinner. But I went anyway, and everything seemed to be okay. The Scribbler was gone, and my desk was all cleaned up. Maybe the Scribbler had changed his mind and decided to go bug some other planet. Maybe Hot Dog could zip right back to Dogzalot and tell the Big Bun that there was no problem down here on Earth after all. Maybe everything was going to go back to nice, boring old normal at Lugenheimer Elementary. Maybe?

Chapter 4

Abnormal Human Beings?

Miss Lamphead gave me a new pencil and let me redo the spelling test. This time the words came out like they were supposed to. But I could hardly breathe for the rest of the day. When the last school bell finally rang, I grabbed my stuff and made for the exit.

"Bob! Wait!" Clementine called. "You gotta fill me in. That wasn't really throw up, was it? Where did you go? Is Hot Dog still in your lunch box? Is everything okay?"

"Evil pencil slime, janitor's closet, unfortunately yes and who knows?" I answered.

"Work with me here, Bob," said Clementine. "A little more information might be helpful."

Since Clementine was the only other person in the world who knew about Hot Dog and remembered the whole horrible Cheese Face incident, I figured she deserved to know. When we got to the sidewalk, away from everybody else, I told her exactly what Hot Dog had told me.

"Oh, no," she said. "Miss Lamphead threw your yucky pencil and paper into the trash can and had Barfalot take it outside. That means—"

"The Scribbler could be anywhere!" I finished.

"We have to tell somebody!" said Clementine.

"No! No! Don't tell!" Hot Dog's muffled voice cried out.

The little guy was jumping and kicking so hard it sounded like someone was popping popcorn in my lunch box. We cracked open the lid to hear what he was saying.

"No one can know," he panted. "This kind of information is simply too much for normal human beings to handle."

"So what does that make Bob and me?" asked Clementine. *"Abnormal* human beings?"

"Well," Hot Dog said. "Let's just say you two aren't exactly *normal."*

"What's *that* supposed to mean?" I demanded.

"Relax, partner, I'm just jokin' around." Hot Dog laughed. "Hey, that's what we partners do. We joke around, right?"

"Oh, yeah, right, good one!" I said, trying to act cool.

But I couldn't help wondering if Hot Dog knew some kind of top-secret information about Clementine and me. I mean, think about it. The Big Bun could have matched Hot Dog up with any partner on the planet. I know I sure wouldn't be *my* first choice if I were looking for some Earthling to help save the world. I was so busy wondering about Hot Dog's "joke" that I didn't even see the water balloons coming.

"Attack the puker!" Barfalot came running from out of nowhere.

"Attack the puker!" repeated his brainless bodyguard brothers, Pigburt and Slugburt.

"Too bad you puked all over the place, and yours truly had to take out your cootie-covered trash," Barfalot blurted as he bombarded me with water balloons.

"Yeah, too bad!" repeated Pigburt and Slugburt.

"You guys are such jerks!" I yelled. "That wasn't even puke! That was—"

"*Nothing!*" Hot Dog yelped from inside my lunch box. "Didn't you hear a word I just said? That is TOP-SECRET INFORMATION!"

Just then a mega-huge water balloon exploded all over Clementine.

"You can stick around if you want to, but I'm outta here!" she said, running away. "Just don't forget to e-mail me tonight. I can't wait to hear how Hot Dog does at your house!"

"My house?" I thought. "Oh, no! I can't take Hot Dog to my house!"

Between my curious parents, my nosy little brother and my hungry basset hound, keeping Hot Dog a secret would be next to impossible. But what choice did I have? I scooped up my lunch box and ran home.

Chapter 5

A Quick Nap

"Wow, you're really wet!" my little brother, Bug, said when I got to my front door. "Why are you so wet?"

"Rain," I answered.

"But it's sunny outside," said Bug.

"An unusual natural weather pattern occurred," I explained. "You'd have to be at least six years old to understand."

"Something's going on," said Bug. "I can tell something's going on."

"*Shhh!* Nothing's going on," I said.

"Oh, yes there is!" said Bug. "Did you do something bad? You did, huh? You *did* do something bad!"

"I'm *gonna* do something bad if you don't quit bugging me!" I threatened.

While Bug went to tell on me (as usual), I went to my room.

"Sheesh!" Hot Dog said when I opened my lunch box. "You people can make skyscrapers

and rocket ships; you'd think you could make a comfortable lunch box."

He was looking a little woozy from all that bouncing around.

"I could be wrong," I said, "but I don't think comfort is really something lunch box makers think about very much."

He climbed out and wobbled around on my bed.

"Not bad," he said, poking my pillow. "This'll do for tonight. But where are you going to sleep?"

"Right here in *my* bed," I said. "It's about a thousand times too big for you!"

"Well that's a fine way to make your partner feel at home!" Hot Dog pouted.

I dumped my card collection out of its shoe box and put in my softest old T-shirt to make a cozy little bed.

"It's not exactly a four-star hotel," said Hot Dog, "but I guess it'll do."

He climbed in and stretched out.

"It's been a big day." He yawned. "If you don't mind, I think I'll take a quick nap."

I hid his little shoe box bed under my big bed and pulled my bedspread all the way down to the floor.

"How's that?" I asked. "Are you comfortable in there?"

I figured the answer was probably yes because all I could hear was snoring. Extremely loud hot-dog snoring.

Juicy Hot Dogs

Dinner that night was a nightmare. Bug kept asking how come I'd come home so wet. He kept saying that he *knew* I was keeping some big, bad secret. I didn't want to lie, but I couldn't tell the entire truth either. Just think what could happen if people found out about Hot Dog. Reporters would follow his every move. Scientists would want to dissect him. And worst of all, the Big Bun would get really mad.

"Hmm, that's funny," said my mom. "I just dropped a piece of potato on the floor and Chomper isn't here to chomp it up."

"I bet the Morrisons are having another one of their famous franks 'n' beans barbecues," said my dad. "Old Chomper probably slipped out the back gate again. It would take an entire army to keep that hound away from those juicy hot dogs!"

"Hot dogs? J-j-juicy h-h-hot dogs?" I said in an embarrassingly high voice. "I'm not feeling very well. May I please be excused?"

When I got to my room, the door was wide open and Chomper's tail was sticking out from under my bed.

Chapter 6

Bad Dog!

"No! Bad dog!" I yelled, pulling Chomper away from the bed. Then I saw it—the terribly empty shoe box. "You ate him! You chomped my partner! How could you do this? The poor little guy didn't even have a chance! What am I going to tell the Big Bun? How am I even going to *find* the Big Bun to tell her?"

I desperately scanned the night-sky poster on my closet door. "Dogzalot, Dogzalot, where are you, Dogzalot?"

"You won't find it there," a voice said. "Dogzalot is in a whole different solar system."

I looked up to see Hot Dog resting comfortably on my windowsill.

"You're alive!" I shouted.

"Okay, okay, keep it down," he said. "You want the whole neighborhood to hear about it? Of course I'm alive! I'm a superhero, for cryin' out loud! It's gonna take a lot more than a saggy old basset hound with halitosis to take me outta this game!"

I gave Hot Dog a great big hug (which, if you've ever tried hugging a hot dog, you'd know isn't the easiest thing to do). Then we sat down on my bed and talked.

"Okay, kiddo," said Hot Dog. "We'd better discuss the plan."

"Right!" I said.

"Right!" Hot Dog said.

"So, what is it?" I asked.

"What is what?" Hot Dog asked.

"The plan," I said. "I thought you wanted to discuss the plan!"

GLITCH

"Oh, right! The plan," said Hot Dog, whose memory had definitely not improved since the *last* time he'd had one of his plans.

"Are you sure we really even need a plan?" I asked. "I mean, if the Scribbler was going to do something awful, wouldn't he have already done it by now?"

"You're gonna have to trust me on this one," said Hot Dog. "We need a plan, and we need it now. There's only one way to get rid of pencil snatchers, and that, my friend, is with a flute!"

"A flute?" I asked.

Hot Dog pointed at the red kazoo on my shelf. "Do you know how to play that thing?"

"Sure," I said.

"It's perfect!" said Hot Dog. "Pencil snatchers have very sensitive ears. They'll follow the sound of the flute like the rats followed the Pied Piper."

"Only one problem," I said. "That's a kazoo, not a flute."

"Don't worry," said Hot Dog. "The kazoo should work fine."

"Should?" I asked.

"Will!" Hot Dog corrected himself. "The kazoo *will* work fine! Okay, here's the plan. I'm gonna set up a sneaky trap. Then you're gonna play the kazoo and lead the pencil snatchers into my sneaky trap. Got it?"

"Are you sure this is going to work?" I asked.

"Sure I'm sure!" said Hot Dog.

I stayed up all night long practicing the kazoo under my covers. In the morning I put it in my pocket and crossed my fingers.

"I sure hope you know what you're talking about," I whispered to Hot Dog as I packed my lunch.

"Relax, buddy," Hot Dog said, getting comfortable next to my bag of carrot sticks. "You do your job, I'll do my job and the world should— I mean *will*—be saved before dinnertime."

Chapter 7

The Art Lesson

When I got to class, Clementine passed me a note that said, "What's up? How come you never e-mailed me last night?"

I wrote back, "I thought Chomper ate Hot Dog, but everything's cool now."

We got our Thursday spelling tests back, and it turned out we all got Fs. Marybell Higgins, who's never gotten less than an A-minus in her life, was so shocked she fainted.

"I could have sworn most of you got As and Bs," Miss Lamphead said, checking her grade book. "Oh, heavens! My grades have all been

 erased and replaced with Fs!
I'm going to take Marybell to
Nurse Bunyan's office. We'll
get to the bottom of this
mystery when I get back."

The second she left, the Scribbler appeared
and jumped on top of Miss Lamphead's desk.

"Things are going to be different around here
now that I'm in charge!" he hollered at the top
of his evil little pencil lungs. "Get out your
pencils for a pop quiz!"

GRRRR

The kids in my class were so surprised they just did just as they were told. But when they reached into their desks, crazy, growling pencils leaped out.

"As you can see, I've made a few changes around here," said the Scribbler. "And I'm about to make a few more. The first pop-quiz question is, Who can guess what the human in the green shirt looks like?"

GRRRRR

We looked over at my friend Marco, and his
pencil was drawing all over him. Before long
he had fur on his face, tons of whiskers and
long tusks.

"Sweet! Marco's a walrus!" exclaimed Barfalot.

"Sweet! Marco's a walrus!" Pigburt and
Slugburt repeated.

"A-plus!" said the Scribbler. "You three must
be the smartest students in this whole class."

"Excellent!" said Barfalot.

"Excellent!" said Pigburt and Slugburt.

It's probably safe to say that that was the first and last time the Terrible Triplets ever got an A on anything.

Marco stood up and tried to take his walrus head off like it was a Halloween mask.

"You're wasting your time." The Scribbler laughed. "We pencil snatchers are master artists. Our work is museum quality and made to last, as in *permanent!*" He looked around. "The next question is, Who can guess what the human in the orange dress is?"

We looked over at Lupi. Her pencil was zipping around her faster than the speed of light.

"Hmm, something fishy's going on around here," mumbled Clementine.

She was right. Lupi had a brand-new, perfectly drawn fish head all covered in shiny scales.

"Can I please go to the drinking fountain?" Lupi asked. "For some reason I just got really thirsty."

The Scribbler ignored her and gave an art lesson to the pencil snatchers instead.

"Better shading! More detail! Are we mere sticks of wood? Or are we the most brilliant artists in the universe? You must practice more, my little scribblers. Practice makes perfect!"

Chapter 8

The Ibblerscray

I used my feet to sneak my lunch box out from under my chair. Then I reached down and flipped up the lid. "Shouldn't we try to stop them?" I whispered. "Hot Dog? Hot Dog, are you in there?"

Hot Dog was snoring away under my carrot sticks. I gave him a poke with my finger.

"Huh? What? Did somebody say something?" he yawned.

"You're *sleeping*?" I yelled as quietly as I could.

Hot Dog rubbed his eyes. "Sorry," he said. "I didn't exactly get the greatest night's sleep with all that kazoo playing, if you know what I mean."

"We're having a little *oblempray* with *the ibblerscray!*" I whispered.

BARFALOT SLUGBURT PiGBURT ROGER

RiCARDO JORDAN

In the little time our short conversation took, the pencil snatchers had already completed their "masterpieces": Barfalot was a bear, Pigburt was a pig, Slugburt was a slug, Felicia was a donkey, Jordan was a lion, Roger was an iguana, José was an ostrich, Ricardo was a cow and Ivy was a chimpanzee.

The Scribbler glared at the pencils that were trying to draw on Clementine and me.

"What's the problem over there?" he asked. "Why haven't you two completed your assignments?"

Our pencils were buzzing around us, looking completely confused. They were drawing and drawing, but nothing was sticking to us.

"Check it out," whispered Clementine. "We're the only ones without animal heads. We're *pencil proof!*"

"Is it you, Hot Dog?" I whispered. "Are you making it so Clementine and I can't get drawn on?"

"I would if I could," said Hot Dog. "I may be a superhero, but I ain't magic!"

"Stop chattering!" the Scribbler yelled. "How am I supposed to concentrate with all that noise? Who do you think you're talking to anyway?"

"Oh, that's just our, uh, imaginary friend!" said Clementine.

"Humans with imaginations?" said the Scribbler. "How unusual. How charming. How possibly *useful!*"

"Useful?" I asked.

"Yes, human in the ugly shirt," the Scribbler answered. "I'm not sure why, I'm not sure how, but something is telling me that you two could assist me in transforming the planet to my liking."

"Your liking?" Clementine asked.

"Yes, human in the pink skirt," said the Scribbler. "This planet is far too crowded. All of your annoying people bodies are cluttering up

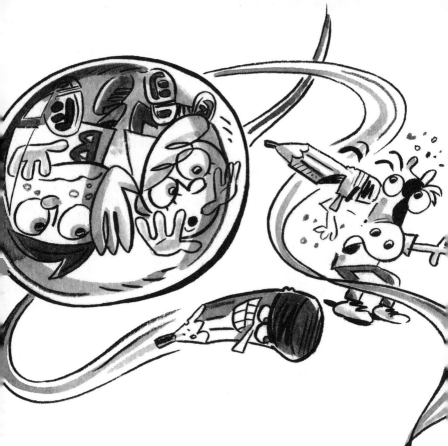

my canvas. My art students and I were just
having a quick little drawing lesson here
before we start erasing."

"Erasing?" I asked.

"Of course," he explained. "In order to create
a true work of art, an artist must begin with a
completely blank canvas. So, as you can see, it
is necessary to erase everything and everybody.

I can't possibly think straight until all of this annoying clutter is gone."

Then he hopped over and scribbled a gigantic bubble around Clementine and me. We were totally trapped. Our poor animal-headed classmates were running around like crazy. The evil pencil snatchers were trying to erase them. And all we could do was sit in our bubble and watch.

Chapter 9

The Plan

"This is a nightmare!" cried Clementine. "We have to stop it! Why won't this stupid bubble pop?"

"Don't worry," I said, reaching into my pocket. "I have a kazoo!"

"That's it?" said Clementine. "A kazoo?"

"This kazoo isn't just any kazoo," I said. "This is *the plan!*"

"About that plan," said Hot Dog. "I'm afraid it's not exactly what you'd call a great trapped-in-a-bubble plan. It's more like a—let's see, how should I put this—*not*-trapped-in-a-bubble plan. Know what I mean, partner?"

Clementine groaned. "Good-bye, sweet world. It was nice knowing you."

"Wait," I said. "If we give up now, the whole world will be erased! There has to be some way to get out of this bubble!"

I searched my backpack, my lunch box and my freaking-out brain for an answer. Finally, at the very bottom of my backpack, I discovered a can of soda pop.

"Purple Blast!" I said.

"*Eww!* You drink that disgusting stuff?" asked Clementine.

"Marco was passing it out after our soccer game last week," I said. "I forgot all about it. If I'm remembering the facts right, there  are enough artificial colors, sweeteners and chemicals in this little can to eat a hole through pretty much anything."

"Including an unpoppable bubble?" said Clementine.

"Hurry up, partner!" said Hot Dog. "Time's a-wastin' and those pencils are erasin'!"

I shook the can of Purple Blast and aimed it at the bubble, and soda pop exploded everywhere.

"It's working!" cheered Clementine. "The bubble is disintegrating!"

The good news was that we were free. The bad news was that we were too late. The only things left of our classmates were pitiful pink piles of eraser dust.

Chapter 9½

Cool Rockin' Tunes

"Now, on to the plan!" I said, pulling out my kazoo. "You make the trap, and I'll lead them into it."

Hot Dog sneakily snuck over to Miss Lamphead's desk. He opened the drawer and filled it with glue. "Do your thing!" he said.

I ran over to the sticky trap and played my kazoo. If the plan worked, the pencil snatchers would follow my music and get stuck in the glue, and the world would be saved. Unfortunately, the pencil snatchers didn't follow my kazoo music at all. They just danced to it!

Chapter 10

Like Roses in Springtime

"Cool rockin' tunes," the Scribbler said. "We could use a little music around here! I knew you would come in handy somehow. And you, human over there in the pink skirt, what useful thing do *you* do?"

Clementine grabbed Hot Dog. Then she started shaking and banging on him like a tambourine.

"Oh, um, I play the hot dog!" she said. "It's a very, uh, *popular* instrument here on Earth!"

Hot Dog yelped as Clementine banged. Between our yelping and kazooing and their

79

dancing, one thing was clear. The pencil snatchers definitely did *not* have supersensitive ears. So much for Hot Dog's plan. We were toast for sure.

"Don't worry," Hot Dog squeaked between the yelps. "I'll think of a new plan any minute!"

Yeah, right. I wasn't exactly getting my hopes up.

"You two can stay until I get tired of your tunes," the Scribbler told us. "After that we'll need to erase you like the others."

When he said "you two" instead of "you three," I realized something. The Scribbler really believed that Hot Dog was just a musical instrument. He had no idea that the yelping thing in Clementine's hands was any kind of superhero at all. I tooted my kazoo and prayed that Hot Dog was going to surprise us with a plan that actually worked—hopefully *soon!*

Meanwhile, the Scribbler and his Pencil Snatchers gang danced and sang.

Erase, erase, erase this world.

Come on, everybody, let's erase this world!

Erase all the boys, erase all the girls.

Yeah, we're gonna scribble up

A whole new world!

I'd always dreamed of playing in a band, but my dream didn't look anything like this.

Then all of a sudden a different sound came out of Hot Dog. It wasn't a yelping sound. It was louder, it was stranger, it was . . . *smellier!*

"Stinkin' sardines!" Clementine gagged. "What died in *your* bun?"

Clementine and I were beyond grossed out by Hot Dog's disgusting fart, but it was worth it. The evil pencils were dropping like flies!

"What's happening?" gagged Clementine. "Are they dying?"

"Pencil snatchers have one great weakness," said Hot Dog. "They have extremely sensitive noses."

"I thought you said they had extremely sensitive *ears!*" I said.

"Ears, noses," said Hot Dog. "There are so many body parts. Can you blame a guy for gettin' them a little mixed up once in a while?"

First of all, the pencil snatchers didn't really have *that* many body parts to get mixed up. Second of all, I *was* blaming Hot Dog. I mean, how hard can it be to remember the one and only incredibly important fact that could save the world?

"Usually they just erase anything that stinks," Hot Dog explained. "But they were so busy singing and dancing they didn't see—er, *smell*—this one comin'! And now, if you'll kindly help me dispose of this mess."

One by one, we stuck the pencils into Miss Lamphead's sharpener and sharpened them

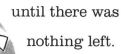 until there was nothing left.

"I don't mean to be ungrateful or anything," said Clementine, plugging her nose. "But do you think you could do something about this smell?"

Hot Dog pushed a secret bun button and sprayed a twinkling mist of flowery-smelling perfume all over the room.

"Ahhh, my favorite scent!" said a voice. "Like roses in springtime!" It was the Scribbler. How could we have forgotten to destroy him?

"Whoops!" said Hot Dog. "Looks like I might have sweetened things up just a little too soon!"

"Oh, I wouldn't say that," the Scribbler said, scribbling thick black lines around Hot Dog. "In fact, I'd say your timing was perfect!"

Chapter 11

Stinky Party Poopers

It's funny how one minute you think your planet is saved and you're going to live happily ever after. Then the next minute your not-so-super superhero partner gets scribbled into a cage. Come to think of it, I guess it's not really that funny after all.

"Run!" Hot Dog yelled. "Save yourselves while you still can!"

"Psst! Bob," Clementine whispered. "Eat this!"

She tossed me the leftover half of her peanut butter, banana, avocado, red pepper, onion, ham, chocolate chip, cream cheese,

raisin, alfalfa sprout and extra hot horseradish on rye bread sandwich. At first I was clueless. But then I understood. Clementine eats radically weird sandwiches every single day of her life, so her stomach is used to the stuff. But my digestive system is used to a simpler diet.

I only eat normal things, like peanuts and pasta. So I don't exactly, uh, *do well* with that kind of unusual food combination.

Clementine's sandwich slid down my throat and landed like a rock in my stomach. Freaky, loud rumbling noises gurgled in my gut. Before long the desired effect of our experiment was produced.

"Jeez Louise!" Clementine gagged as she was blown over by my stinky blast of wind. "I take it back! I choose the end of the world!"

"Look!" I said, pointing at the Scribbler, who was rolling around on the floor.

"Phooey! You stinky party poopers!" He gasped. "This planet could have been so beautiful! It could have been my greatest masterpiece! You've ruined everythingggg!"

And that was that. He couldn't handle the smell of the gas I'd passed for one more second. He was a lifeless little stick of wood, just exactly like a pencil is supposed to be.

"Fantastic!" said Hot Dog.

"Yes!" Clementine and I said, high-fiving each other with one hand and holding our shirts over our noses with the other.

It took a while to erase a big enough hole in the cage for Hot Dog to squeeze out, but we did it. Then we sharpened the Scribbler into nothingness. Don't ask me how, but as soon as the Scribbler was gone, our classmates reappeared.

"Sick!" said Barfalot. "Who cut the cheese?"

"It's sad," sighed Clementine. "He was so much more pleasant when he was a pile of eraser dust."

"Pleasure workin' with you, as always," Hot Dog said with a salute.

"I'll see you on our next mission!"

And then it was total déjà vu. Just like last time, Hot Dog pushed his secret everybody-forgets-everything magic-sparkle rain-shower button and disappeared into thin air. And just like last time, his mysterious forgetting shower worked on everybody but Clementine and me. *We* got to remember every single sick, slimy, scribbly detail.

Just then Miss Lamphead and Marybell returned. "You'll all be delighted to know Nurse

Bunyan says Marybell is going to be fine," Miss Lamphead announced as she opened the door.

I looked around the classroom. It was so weird, like no time had passed at all. All the kids were sitting at their desks with people heads instead of animal heads. They were holding regular pencils instead of scary evil alien ones. And nobody but Clementine and me had any idea that the world had been moments away from being completely erased forever.

THE END
(for now)

As an award-winning investigative reporter specializing in extraterrestrial activity, **L. Bob Rovetch** has spent hundreds of hours interviewing Bob and helping him record his amazing but true adventures. Ms. Rovetch lives across the Golden Gate Bridge from San Francisco with two perfect children and plenty of pets.

Dave Whamond wanted to be a cartoonist ever since he could pick up a crayon. During math classes he would doodle in the margin of his papers. One math teacher warned him, "You'd better spend more time on your math and less time cartooning. You can't make a living drawing funny pictures." Today Dave has a syndicated daily comic strip, called *Reality Check*. Dave has one wife, two kids, one dog, and one kidney. They all live together in Calgary, Alberta.

Look Out!
The Hypno Hamsters and Gutter Gators Are Heading Your Way!

Just when you thought the world was safe! Arriving in Spring 2007 are two new Hot Dog and Bob adventures.

Hot Dog and Bob and the Hypno Hamsters

It's Career Day at Lugenheimer Elementary School, but when one parent arrives to talk about being a toy maker, things start to go mysteriously wrong. Will Hot Dog and Bob be able to stop plush hamsters from taking over the world? Will Clementine ever be able to look at hamsters and their darling exercise wheels again? Find out in the next installment of Hot Dog and Bob.

Hot Dog and Bob and the Gutter Gators

Bob, Clementine and Miss Lamphead's entire class from Lugenheimer Elementary School find themselves transported to the domain of the Gutter Gator— perhaps their most far-out adversary yet. Will Bob and Clementine find their way out of the gators' maze in time to save the world? Will Hot Dog find his way to his partner when Bob needs him most? Stay tuned!

- Verify that the bank processed all of your deposits when they should have. If the bank delayed processing a deposit, you should not have to pay a fee.
- Verify that the checks that cleared were "encoded" for the right amount. It's fairly rare, but it can happen that a bank will process a $100 check for $1000. That can make a big difference to your balance.

If the bounced check wasn't your fault and the bank made the mistake, don't just settle for a refund of the charges they made. Your bank should be willing to write a letter to the person or company who deposited your check, telling them that the return was an error on the bank's part and not your fault. If your bank won't do this for you, seriously consider getting another bank!

Consider Overdraft Protection

One way to cover yourself in the event you write a check that bounces is to sign up for overdraft protection. This allows you a line of credit (up to a specified amount) that covers checks written against insufficient funds.

You will not incur a returned check charge with overdraft protection, but you will pay interest on the amount accessed on the line of credit until you pay it back. Usually, if you pay the amount back as soon as the bank notifies you, the amount of interest you must pay is lower than the returned check charge—and less hassle.

Overdraft protection should be used only in an emergency or in some organized fashion with a payback plan in mind. Don't use it frequently as a substitute for a regular line of credit since you may run out of credit just when you need it to cover a true overdraft!

don't be afraid to approach your bank about the problem. The branch representative will not automatically assume that you are a deadbeat just because you made a mistake. Second, point out to the banker that it took (usually) two or three days from the time the account was overdrawn for them to notify you of the fact, and for you to even have a chance of taking action. You may question whether you should have to pay all of these fees before you had a chance to do something about them. Third, don't hesitate to use the other account relationships you have with the bank to negotiate away some, or all, of the bounced check fees.

While there are relatively few times that you will be able to actually "cut a deal" with your banker, overdraft charges may be one of those times. This is especially true if your bank has high fees and charges per check returned. Total overdraft fees of $75-150 from one incident are not unusual if you actively use your checking account and frequently have more than one check clearing per day.

Many branch representatives are actually embarrassed by the amount of fees that accumulate. If they believe you corrected the problem as soon as you could and know that you have other account relationships with them that they could lose if they don't treat you right, you can often negotiate the fees. You probably won't escape all of the charges, but many times you can get the branch manager to waive all but, say, one fee per day. There's no guarantee that he will negotiate, but it's worth a try.

Finally, banks can make mistakes, too. When you bounce a check, find out for sure if it was your fault: